A Hippopotamus Ate the Teacher

30th Anniversary Edition

by Mike Thaler

Illustrated by Jared Lee

SCHOLASTIC INC.

New York   Toronto   London   Auckland

Sydney   Mexico City   New Delhi   Hong Kong

To Doug and Diana Quaid—
Always close at heart.
—M.T.

Rarely does one get the opportunity to re-illustrate a book they
did thirty years ago. With that said, I dedicate this revised
version to its original editor, Jean Feiwel.
—J.L.

ISBN 978-0-545-35707-4

Text copyright © 1981 by Mike Thaler
Illustrations copyright © 2011 by Jared D. Lee Studio, Inc.

12 11 10 9 8   12 13 14 15 16/0

Originally published by Avon Camelot, September 1981

Printed in the U.S.A.   40

First Scholastic printing, September 2011

One day our teacher, Ms. Jones, took us to the zoo.

She showed us the monkeys,

the tigers,

and the kangaroo.

Then she showed us
the hippopotamus.

But she leaned too close to
the rail to feed it a peanut

and she fell in

and the hippopotamus ate her!

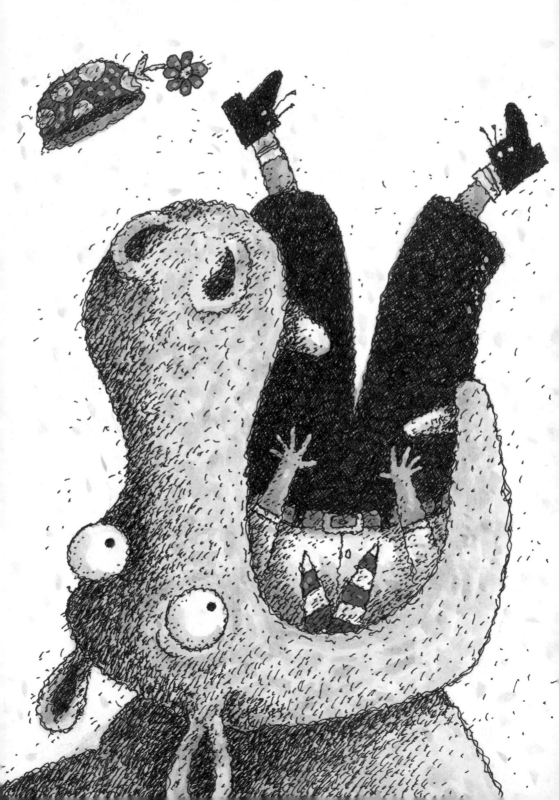

"Oh my!" we all cried. We went to the zookeeper and told him, "The hippopotamus just ate our teacher."

"Oh my!" said the zookeeper.

He went to the zoo director.

"The hippopotamus just ate their teacher."

"Oh my!" said the zoo director.

We went to the hippopotamus.

The zoo director opened up the
hippopotamus's mouth and we
all looked in. But we couldn't
see anything.

Then all of a sudden a voice came from deep inside the hippopotamus. "All right, class, it's time to go," said the voice.

It was Ms. Jones!

"Line up and hold hands," said the voice from inside the hippopotamus. So we did.

"Follow me back to the bus," said the voice. So we did.

Then the whole class rode back
to school with the hippopotamus.

The other teachers were very
surprised when we all arrived.

The principal was very surprised also.
But we explained it to him.

So the next day the hippopotamus taught our class.

It taught us math

and history

and geography.

It read us stories.

All the other kids thought the hippopotamus was great. They looked in the windows and peeked in the door. But as time went on we began to miss Ms. Jones.

It was hard to hug the hippopotamus
and we couldn't sit on its lap.

So one day in the middle of a history lesson we all grabbed the hippo and turned it upside down.

Then we shook it till Ms. Jones fell out.

"Well, class," she said. "Back to your seats."

"The third president of the United States was Thomas Jefferson."

"Any questions?" She smiled, adjusting her glasses.